E
Gl   Glen, Maggie

       Ruby

cl

DEMCO

Ruby

*For Ellie, Naomi, Roddy
and special bears everywhere*

♥

First American Edition published
in 1991 by G. P. Putnam's Sons,
a division of the Putnam & Grosset Book Group,
200 Madison Avenue, New York, NY 10016.
Originally published in 1990 by
Hutchinson Children's Books, London.

Printed in Belgium
Typography by Kathleen Westray

Library of Congress Cataloging-in-Publication Data
Glen, Maggie.
Ruby / Maggie Glen.—1st American ed.
p.   cm.   "Originally published in 1990 by
Hutchinson Children's Books, London"—T.p. verso.
Summary: Ruby, a teddy bear accidentally made out of the wrong
material, leads other rejected toy bears in an escape from the
toy factory and seeks a place where she will be appreciated.
[1. Teddy bears—Fiction.   2. Prejudices—Fiction.]   I. Title.
PZ7.G48285Ru 1991   [E]—dc20   90-38903   CIP AC
ISBN 0-399-22281-2
1 3 5 7 9 10 8 6 4 2
First American Edition

Ruby

MAGGIE GLEN

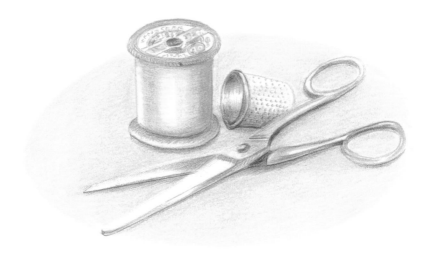

G. P. PUTNAM'S SONS
New York

*R*uby felt different from other bears—sort of special.

Mrs. Harris had been daydreaming when she made Ruby. She didn't notice that she was using the spotted material that was meant for the toy leopards. She didn't watch carefully when she sewed on the nose.

Ruby wasn't surprised when she was chosen from the other bears, but she didn't like being picked up by her ear.

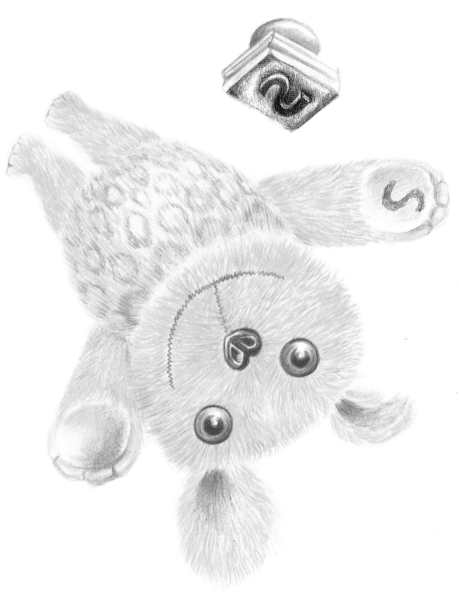

"OUCH, GET OFF!" she growled.
Ruby's paw was stamped with an "S" and
she was thrown into the air.
"YIPPEE-E-E-E! 'S' IS FOR SPECIAL," Ruby yelled.

Ruby flew across the factory and landed in a box full of bears.
"Hello," she said. "My name's Ruby and I'm special—see." She held up her paw.

"No, silly," laughed a big bear. "'S' is for 'second'—second best."

"We're mistakes," said the bear with rabbit ears. "When the box is full, we'll be thrown out."

Ruby's fur stood on end. She was horrified.

More bears joined them in the box.

At last the machines stopped. The bears listened to the workers as they chatted and hurried to catch the bus home. They heard the key turn in the lock. Then everything was quiet. One by one they fell asleep.

All except Ruby—Ruby was thinking. All she could hear was the sound of the big bear snoring.

Hours passed. Suddenly Ruby shouted, "That's it!"

"What's it?" gasped the rabbit-eared bear, who woke up with a fright.

"Zzzzzzzzzzzzzzzzzz-w-w-what's going on?" groaned the big bear, rubbing his sleepy eyes.

"That's *it*," Ruby said again. "We'll escape."

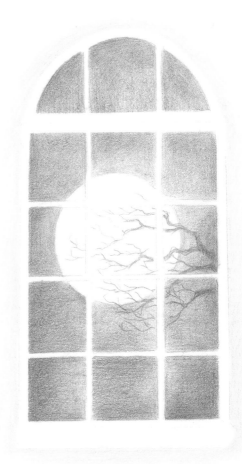

"ESCAPE!" they all shouted. And they jumped out of the box.

"Let's go!" said Ruby.

They looked for a way out.
They rattled the windows.
They pushed at the doors.
"There *is* no way out," cried a little bear.
"We're trapped."
"This way," Ruby shouted, rushing into
the rest room.

They found a broken air vent.
It was a very tight squeeze.
They pushed and they pulled,
they wiggled and they waggled,
until they were all in the yard outside.

They ran silently, swiftly, through the night and into the day.

Some ran to the country, some to the town.

Some squeezed through mail slots.   Some slipped through open windows.

Some hid in toy cupboards.

Some crept into bed with lonely children.

But Ruby . . .

. . . climbed into the window of the very best toy shop in town.

The other toys stared at Ruby.
"What's the 'S' for?" squealed the pigs.
"Special," said Ruby proudly.
All the toys shrieked with laughter.
"Scruffy," said the smart-looking penguin.
"Soppy," said the chimpanzee.
"Stupid," giggled the mice.
"Very strange for a bear," they all agreed.

"Don't come next to me," said a prim doll.
"Wouldn't want to," Ruby said.
"Stand at the back," shouted the other toys.
They poked, they pulled, they prodded and they pinched.
Ruby pushed back as hard as she could, but there were
too many of them.

So Ruby spent all day at the back of the shelf.

Then, just before closing time, a small girl came into the shop with her grandfather.

They searched and searched for something—something different, something special.

"That's the one," the little girl said.

"Yes, Susie," said Grandfather, "that one looks very special."

Ruby looked around her. "Can they see me?"
"We'll have that one, please," said Grandfather.

"IT'S ME! They're pointing at me. WHOOPEE-E-E-E!"

The shopkeeper put Ruby on the counter.
She looked at the "S" on Ruby's paw. "I'm sorry, sir," she said.
"This one is a second. I'll get another one."

"No, thank you, that one is just perfect," said Grandfather. "It has character."

Character, thought Ruby, that sounds good.

"Shall I wrap it for you?" the shopkeeper asked.

"Not likely," Ruby growled. "Who wants to be shoved inside a paper bag?"

"No, thank you," Susie said. "I'll take her just as she is."

They all went out of the
shop and down the street.
When they came to a
yellow door they stopped.
"We're home, Spotty,"
Susie said.
"Spotty, what a joke!"
Ruby muttered.
"It's got a growl," Susie
said, and she and her
grandfather laughed.

Susie took off her coat and scarf, and set Ruby on her lap.

Susie stared at Ruby and Ruby stared back.

Suddenly, Ruby saw a little silver "S" hanging on a chain around Susie's neck.

Hooray! thought Ruby. Susie's one of us—a special.